Billy the Baaad Goat in

The Big Yellow Rocket Ship

Wishing you
great fun
and learning?

Cheers!
Grampa
Mitch

By Mitch A. Lewis
Illustrations: Stefanie St. Denis
and Leeah Jo Houston-Rellamas

Tellwell Talent
www.tellwell.ca

ISBN
978-0-2288-3054-2 (Hardcover)
978-0-2288-3053-5 (Paperback)
978-0-2288-3055-9 (eBook)

To Clara and Lucy,
I can't wait to see what moons and planets you'll discover!
- Grampa Mitch

Part One:
Billy the Dreamer

ONCE UPON A TIME there was a goat named William;

Billy, as he was called, marched to a different drum.

Strawberry Fields[1] was the name of his home-farm.

Since forever, the Fields had a magical charm.

Billy lived there with Farmer John and Farmher Joan.

All his animal friends were there too.

And on this farm was a big red barn.

Which was called the *Animal House*.

Where all the critters lived, even the cows!

(Now, Strawberry Fields was no ordinary farm.

It had talking goats,

The chimps would eat the oats,

And no one would ever bite or cause harm.)

On normal farms you won't find

Lions, tigers, or bears,

Giraffes, or monkeys of any kind,

But using our imagination

Helps us find our DETERMINATION!

Farmer John and Farmher Joan

Lived in a cabin built of logs.

Though it was old and brown,

Norwegian Wood[2] kept out storms and dogs;

"Not in the house," they would smile-frown.

Grains and fruits and vegetables they did grow,

Even wheat to bake their own bread.

With the tractor they did sow;

Their strawberries were always the brightest red.

Farmer John and Farmher Joan are farmers now,

but they used to live in Oakland City.

She was an astrophysicist who was smart and gritty.

He hoped to trade software programming for a plow.

One day, after the virus passed,

And they could at long last put away their masks,

They decided to move away from the cars and traffic and noise;

To live in nature with own-grown fruits and vegetables and soy.

At first, they worried about no office or a local store,

But soon, they came to love their animals and crops even more.

Laughing and learning and studying, their hearts could finally soar.

For all the creatures the New Farmers came to deeply adore.

Strawberry Fields was an incredibly
happy place indeed!

Billy Goat Tavern

ENTER AT YOUR OWN RISK

MENU

Billy, even as a little one, got into trouble a lot;

He was always poking his Billy-goat-beard into things he should not.

Billy came to the farm

When he was just a kid.

His goat-parents lived nearby

With some friendly farmers

Who had lots of grass to rid.

Billy was kinda baaad no matter what he did.

He'd nose around the trash,

And kick the can down the road from his stash.

He even got blamed for a baseball team losing long ago,

(But they named a tavern after him in Chi-ca-go[3]).

Billy had a good heart and was mostly glaaad

As anyone would duly note.

But sometimes he was baaad.

After all, he was a goat!

And that's how he became known as Billy the Baaad Goat.

When Billy got maaad,

He said things he didn't mean.

And little things sometimes made him mean,

And some things made him want to scream!

While playing with his friends,

For a minute, he'd lose his kind-mind,

And he'd say something baaad,

Like he'd gone momentarily blind.

Later... he'd be maaad at himself for getting maaad!

The animals he voice-hurt did not soon forget they were then-saaad.

Some animals made fun of Billy because he wanted to explore.

He so loved music and big books and was curious to his core.

Farmer John and Farmher Joan would croon to Billy every night.

They would sing him songs under the night-light

About ancient dinosaurs, modern astronauts,

Mysterious lands, and faraway planets.

These story-songs made Billy want to learn more about everything.

Curiosity for him was never just a fling.

He learned that ants sting

After he poked his nose in a red-ant hill; he didn't do that again!

One day, Billy was sitting on a rock

Near the *Dock Of The Bay*[4].

He felt *The Warmth of the Sun*[5].

And thought of the things he wanted to get done.

Rita the Rabbit, chewing a carrot, started to mock,

And said, "'What's up, Doc?[6]

Billy, you're such a dreamer.'"

"'I may be a dreamer,

But I'm Not the Only One,'"[7]

He replied under his tongue.

Billy the Baaad Goat was dreaming about going into space
In a rocket ship!
In a race,
On a trip,
To the Moon,
But with whom!!

He wanted to go the Moon, but with whom and how?!

In the middle of a large Strawberry Field, was a very tall spaceship.
Farmer John had called it his *Field of Dreams*[8], from a movie-clip.
Farmher Joan had spent the last three years building the ship.
She designed it to go on a Moon-Trip.
And had built the Big Yellow Rocket Ship[9] for just such a trick.

Billy saw the giant rocket and stopped in place...
He had long-plan-dreamed of flying into space!

He gathered his animal friends and presented a choice.

"Aaanyone waaant to go to the Moon?" he

shouted in his uneven goat-voice.

All the animals came a-runnin' or they flew.

Billy looked at their faces and knew what to do;

He gave all the animals chores to make them part of the crew.

All had much to prepare besides their feed.

Everyone had to know about rules and safety and speed,

The motors, power, and steering – everything they'd need.

Billy united his friends for the team that he would lead.

He put on his spacesuit for the first time and went to show the rest;

He was so happy and couldn't wait to prove he could be the best,

But some of them made fun of him and called him a big pest.

Bluesy the Blue Jay chirped in his ear, "You

can't do this. You're no good."

That made Billy saaad.

Then, Henry the Horse brayed, "You can't even dance a waltz.[10]"

This made Billy maaad.

Billy bleated, "'You don't get time to

hang a baaad sign on me.'"[11]

Just then, Rocky Raccoon burst in, and though grinning a grin[12],

He himself was not without sin.

Rocky could tell Billy was saaad,

Though Rocky was usually pretty glaaad.

"Listen," Rocky said, "'who put all those things in your head?'"[13]

Roxy the Raccoon chipped in, "I know what it's like to be in dread.

It's OK to be scared,

Of what you've been dared."

You need DETERMINATION.

(It's a big word, but it means not giving up, no matter what.)

Do you know what I mean?" she asked in anticipation.

Billy thought for a minute. "I think so," he guessed.

"When I find a boot that's really tough, but I have to chew my best?"

Roxy gave a splendid clap.

Gideon the Giraffe had taught him that!

"'Everyone thinks I'm lazy;'"

Billy said, "'I think they're crazy.[14]

Sometimes for me, things can get a bit hazy.

But if I seem to act unkind,

It's only me; it's not my mind.'"[15]

"We get it," Rocky and Roxy together chimed.

Now Billy was determined.

Remembering all he knew,

About rocket ships and outer space from school,

As the captain, he could show his crew,

That he too could be cool.

Billy called his space crew together in the control room.
Before he began, he chewed on a broom.
He did this a lot when he worried about doom.
He felt excited and scared about zooming to the Moon!

Billy said, "OK, friends, we're going 'Aaacross the Universe'[16]!
Or at least to the Moon.
Whooo's In? We're leaving sooon!"

All the animals started to bark, squeak, chirp, and more.
Lucy the Lioness released a giant roar!

"Let's rock-it!" Billy said. "I have no fear!"
(He did try to hide a single scaredy tear.)

They'd all go to sleep and then meet at dawn.

By now, Billy had seen many a yawn.

Tomorrow they would Zoom,

To the faraway Moon!

And without a peep,

They all fell fast asleep.

Their dreams they would soon meet.

zzzzzzzzz [End Part One] zzzzzzzzz

Part Two:
Blast-Off

On 'Wednesday morning at 5 o'clock'[17],

Randy Rooster and Helda the Hen awakened

them with their cock-a doodle-doos.

The fowls seemed especially foul today and none got to snooze.

All of Billy's animal friends were there to see

them off on their rocket-cruise.

Some had to stay behind – on a farm there are many to-dos!

They brought spacesuits, water, and food for the skies.

Like Rocky's favorite, "Marshmallow Pies"[18],

Which he liked much better than Farmer

John's "Fish and Finger Pies".[19]

Yuckify!

Billy waved goodbye, stepped inside, and closed the door.

With his co-pilots, Rocky and Vera the Viper, they would soon soar.

They started up the Big Yellow Rocket Ship.

Pushing buttons and pulling dials with a tight grip.

Suddenly...
ALL THE LIGHTS started to turn on by design:
Red, yellow, and green colors and tick-tock sounds.
Buzzers, beeps, and bongs!
And a countdown clock with very loud gongs!
5 – 4 – 3 – 2 – 1...

BLAST-OFF!!!

THE BIG YELLOW ROCKET SHIP lifted off
with "Great Balls of Fire" galore.[20]
There would be so much to explore.
The force of the power to leave Earth and soar,
Pushed their buns deep into the seats.
Even the chicks couldn't tweet their peeps!

Soon it was so quiet. After leaving Earth's gravity,
They entered the troposphere place.
Billy thought it was "The Sound of Silence"[21] in Space.
(Space has no sound.)
Sassy Squirrel thought the sky was "Paint It, Black."[22]
(Not at all like it is from the ground.)

Billy knew from his books that the Moon is about 250,000 miles away.
"How faaaar is that?" he paused to wonder,
Pulling on his luscious goat-beard.
He did some arithmetic without blunder,
Pulling up data that had been brain-seared.
The number would be no wonder.

"3,000 miles to Grandma and Grandpa's
house in six hours is a math-game.
3,000 divided by six equals five-hundred
miles-per-hour in an aero-plane
When Farmer John and Farmher Joan travel to see their kin.
Can we go any faster so we can get back before din-din?"

Vera'd been studying rocket science and
said, "I know how!" with a scold.
"We have to go more than 25,000 miles an
hour to break Earth's gravity hold.
If we go that speed till we get there, it will only take 10 hours!"

"We can get back in less than one day?
Aaawesome!" Billy said with a noisy bray!

Rocky set a course for the moon and all the
animals settled in for the ride.

"The stars are sparkling like Diamonds," Lucy sighed.
"Yes," Clara the Calico Cat meowed. "I see Marmalade Skies."[23]

They both giggled with laughs and dancing twirls!
Barbara the Bear snorted and said, "Funny Girls!"[24]

Billy was "Keeping an Eye on the World
Going by His Window".[25]

SUDDENLY THERE IT WAS! The Moon!

They'd looked at it every night since they could remember.
At times, it was full in December;
Sometimes, it was only half-full like an eye;
And sometimes, it looked like a slice of 'butter-pie'[26].

All the animals knew when the Moon was full
and bright; some even liked to howl!
"Owwwwooooooo" Warren the Wolf and
his wife Wanda started to growl!

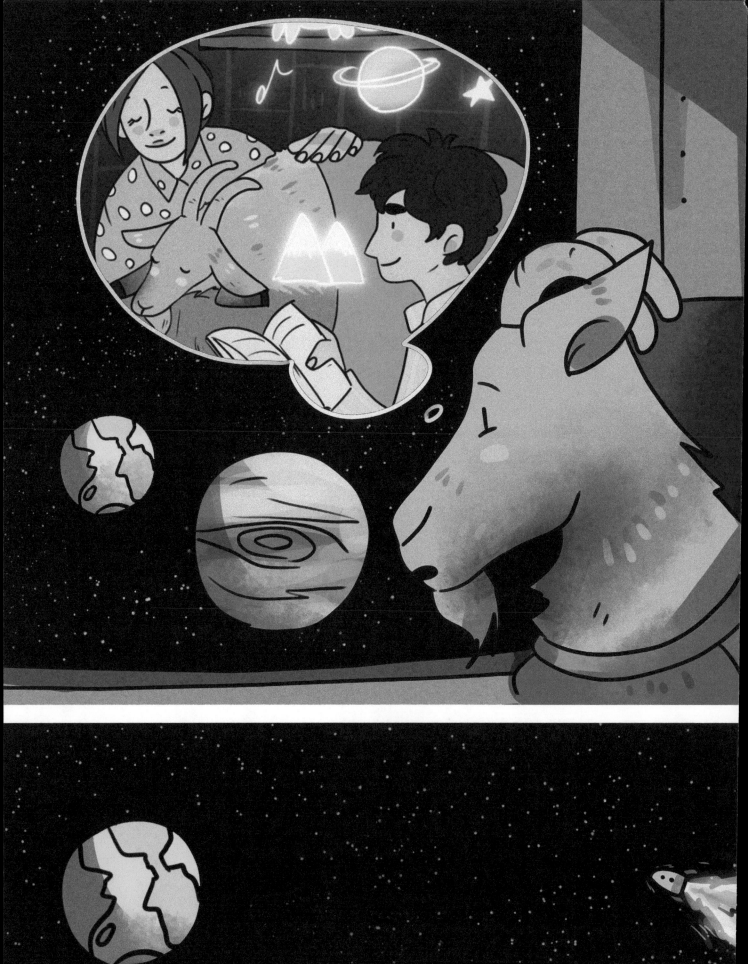

Farmer John had told Billy that the Moon

made the waves in the ocean.

He had said it's because of the Moon's pulling motion.

"Aaamazing!" Billy said, and he remembered this poem:

"This Cold-Hearted Orb That Rules the Night,

Removes the Colors from our Sight."[27]

He <u>did</u> see colors through his window,

The Earth's hue was like Dodger-Blue.

And even though he loved his crew,

He missed his family back home,

For they were all that he ever knew.

Now Billy had to focus, for in orbit around the Moon they were.

"Wherrre should we land?" he asked with a grrr.

Chuck the Chimp got an idea while riding his exercise bike;

"Why don't we land near the top of the Moon

and see what the North Pole is like?

We can jump and play in the snow with our paws,

Maybe there's even a Moon Santa Claus!"

Harvey the Hyena fell on his back and laughed,

"No Santa Claus here, ha-ha-ha!"

Time to land the Big Yellow Rocket Ship on the Moon!

DAVE THE DINGO said, "Good on you, mate.

I'll get the spacesuits ready."

Vera reminded everyone about the dangers of space,

"Remember, there's no air to breathe; and

it's very cold <u>and</u> hot in this place."

"How cold is it?" Edd the Eel[28] said and heard a thump.

(Somewhere a snare-drum had announced, "*padump-bump*.")

"Well," Vera said, "it can get down to two-
hundred and fifty degrees below zero.
Almost anything can freeze within seconds, you should know.
We have to wear our spacesuits, and don't say no."

Chuck swung over, and while hanging upside-down, foretold:
"Besides having no good air, and it being very cold,
We won't weigh much compared to Earth by and by.
So be careful not to bounce too high!"

Billy couldn't wait to bounce-play with his friends!

Molly the Monkey got ready to land the Big Yellow Rocket Ship.

They were going to land near the top of the

Moon - known as the polar ice cap!

She blasted the jets and they made a soft-sand landing in a snap.

They looked outside to see if there were any

"Strangers in this Strange Land".[29]

They were alone, and it was grand.

Billy had always stared at the Man-in-the-

Moon and assumed it was a man

Though he couldn't possibly understand.

Till he once asked Gideon why the same Moon

face always stared the same way.

The giraffe, as he chewed some leaves,

explained to Billy and the Blue Jay:

"The Moon takes 27 days to turn like a top,

And 27 days to go 'round the Earth nonstop.

Like two people turning the same two pots,

In a way, it's like the Moon's always facing the same spots!"

"How weird and interesting!" Billy thought.

Everyone wanted to go outside and play!

Bluesy, Redd Robin, and Bella the Blackbird couldn't wait to fly.
Molly and Chuck were jumping and fighting by and by.
Clara and Lucy were rolling 'round the floor, having fun; oh my!

Outside they went!

Many started to play; some went exploring.
(Not a one was now snoring!)
They left their footprints in the Moon-dust,
As they shook off some spaceship rust.

Sassy the Squirrel chirped, "There's no ice, snow, or water here."
"Why not?" Clara asked and waited to hear.

"Problem is," Sassy started, "no atmosphere on the Moon."
(These are air layers above the Earth that
protect us from certain doom.)
"On Earth, the atmosphere keeps our oceans and lakes from drying up."
"Hmmm," Billy thought, "Could Moon-water
help fill the world's drinking cup?"

Billy the Baaad Goat went exploring.

He bounded happily between craters, over
rocks, and above giant cracks.
Then he looked closely. "What is it?" Rocky said, thinking of snacks.
"It's maaaybe some Moon ice-rocks. We have time to grab..."
Just then their phone-radios started
beeping loudly; it sounded baaad.

"CAPTAIN, WE HAVE A PROBLEM!"

Chuck chirped into the phone-radio.

("It better not

Be Houston," Sassy thought.)[30]

"WE HAVE TO LEAVE RIGHT NOW;
Our oxygen is getting low.
Plus, we have to go home;
We're all feeling so alone."

"OK," Billy said. "Back to the ship everyone. Hurry-hurry!
Lack of air could make our vision quite blurry."
Just then his paw kicked a mound of something.
He had found some ice-rocks he thought he should bring.

Now came the hardest part:
Getting back to the start.

Billy missed Farmer John and Farmher Joan.
Trouble always made the farmers groan
They unconditionally loved him very much,
Even when he got into goat-trouble as such.

As the Big Yellow Rocket Ship blasted off, they all looked down.
All the animals heaved a giant moan.
Now... they were "On The Way Home."[31]

Just as they started to leave,
Came flashing lights and wailing sirens they could not believe.

BANG! WHOOSH! WEE-OWW!
Something had gone wrong; how would
they ever get back now??!!

zzzzzzzzzz [End Part Two] zzzzzzzzzz

Part Three:
No Place Like Home

The alarms kept Billy from his nap-song;

He knew something was wrong.

"What happened?" he wondered. "Something's amiss;

Did I do this?"

With newspapers to chew,

and tin cans to kick,

He had to fix the ship,

Before everyone turned blue.

A small meteor had hit the ship, he figured out.

Though the hole was super-small, he knew that's not what it's about;

Even a tiny hole would drain oxygen from the ship.

Oh no! This was no tiny blip.

As the crew turned to Billy, he wasn't the least bit sussed,

For in his scientist, Vera, he did trust.

"Yes," she did hiss, "I know what's required."

Her long forked-tongue slipped into a grin.

"I need to 'fix a hole where the air gets in

And stop the ship from wanderin'."[32]

Though a little scared herself, she had the education,

Which helped Vera gain DETERMINATION.

With some Gorilla-Glue and Duck-Tape, her ideas had no bounds!

All the animals cheered for her with their "Pet Sounds"![33]

"YAKETY-YAK[34], LET'S GO BACK!"

They all screamed with joy;

"We're back on track!"

They'd be back soon to munch their bok choy.

Soon, Earth came into view and it got bigger
and bigger in the rocket dome.
Back in radio contact, he was now able to 'Phone Home'.[35]

Billy remembered he had forgotten to tell
The farmers where they were going.
He had no way of knowing
If they would want to yell.

Billy got Farmer John on the radio-screen.
He told of what happened without lies.
Farmer John was as forgiving as he was wise.
"Just get home safely," he said with kind-eyes.

Just as the hardest part of any mountain is getting safely down,
A rocket has to slow and brake or get blown.
All because the atmospheric resistance causes a heat-crown.

Billy, Rocky, and Vera would have to
cooperate to come home.
They needed Team-Work or no oxygen
could cause their mouths to foam.

At school, Billy didn't always place nice.

Sometimes he'd eat their books or kick their toys.

It might have been too much sugar in his pies

That made him lose it with the other boys.

Born in the Black Mountain Hills,

Rocky was at best, rambunctious.

He once got in a fight with Dan over unpaid bills,

Later, he said to the doc, "It's only a scratch."[36]

Vera was mostly very sweet in her lair-patch;

Most days, there was no victim to bite-scratch.

She liked to sit on her Mimi's lap with Chuck and Dave.[37]

But sometimes she'd get mad and hiss when she had a crave.

Billy said, "We must all collaborate, is my advice."

They all nodded their heads and smiled.

Today, they would all play nice.

Fire and flame as the ship came down;

The crew was acting all grown.

Billy felt like Ethan the Elephant was on his chest,

But he still tried to do his best.

And then, they were floating on an orange parachute.

Rocky steered the ship.

With eyes closed, Billy got the landing gear down without a blip,

And Vera fixed the speed without a slip.

5 - 4 - 3 - 2 - 1
A soft bump. Touchdown!

Had Billy really flown a rocket ship to the Moon and back?

Or was he dreaming?

When he opened his eyes,

He could not believe what he was seeing!

In the middle of the strawberry field where they departed,

Were the animals who stayed behind.

From where they'd been parted,

Was a big crowd,

And it was so loud,

And they were all cheering and being kind!

"Let's all yell Hip-Hip-Hooray!"
The other animals said with a loud imitation bray!

As slow as a Moon-rover,

Paul-is-the-Walrus[38] waddled over.

To give Billy the "thumbs-up" with his enormous flipper.

Oh – the after-party would be quite a ripper!

Then Billy saw a big sign:
WELCOME HOME
To be home again was quite divine.

Farmer John and Farmher Joan ran to hug Billy.

He put his head and horns in their loving arms,

And expressed his sorrow for setting off the alarms.

In the morning cold,

Bluesy and Henry came up to Billy.

They could not believe he could be so bold!

They were twittering and neighing and not being silly,

Though they were anyway quite chilly.

"We're sorry we were mean to you. We should have been more kind,

Will you forgive us for not being then of sound mind?"

"Of course." Their sorry's he did accept.

This was something Billy could not reject.

He too apologized for being baaad and mean,

Billy would try harder to be nice and clean.

He then boasted, "You know what G.O.A.T. means?
The Greatest Of All Time – that's Billy!"
They all smiled and thought it was not-silly.

It was bedtime for Billy and all the animals.

"Billy," Farmer John said (though Billy knew),

"What you did today was bad; we'll have to punish you.

You're grounded for one month – that'll do."

"But," Billy butted in,

Farmer John quickly shushed him.

"Time to go night-night,

It's been a long day."

Then Billy saw something in his night-sight,

He remembered the ice-rocks he had brought home from a long way.

Farmer John started to speak,

"You found frozen water on the Moon?

The future is maybe not so bleak.

Mankind needs more water on Earth or else constant drought-gloom,

Perhaps big rocket ships could bring us ice-

water in less than a week?!"

"The solution would certainly be unique.

For being clever, I'm reducing your punishment to one week.

But still no *Netflix* on your *iPad*,

Even if you act all sad."

"Yes," Billy agreed. "I'll continue to learn and grow."

"Very good, we love you very much. Now go to sleep,

Without a single bleat.

Yesterday is done, but tomorrow we'll never know."[39]

The farmers turn, turn, turned[40] out the

lights and quietly closed the door.

They could soon hear his rumbling goat-snore.

They smiled at each other and did some guessin',

"I sure hope he learned his lesson."

They winked, but they knew better...

Billy later woke in his bed after a time,
Chewing his paper and tin can pasie; he was in his prime.
In a very scary situation,
Billy had found DETERMINATION.

"Hmmmmm," he thought just before he fell deeply asleep,
"I've got an idea," he thought, just as dreams did creep.
"A Green Submarine could go very deep...!!"

Billy was soon in Dreamland,
With his dream-plans.

zzzzzzzzzz [The End] zzzzzzzzzz

Cast of Characters

Starring: Billy the Baaad GOAT
Co-starring: Farmer JOHN and Farmher JOAN
Supported by: Rocky and Roxy RACCOON
Plus: Clara the CALICO CAT and Lucy the LIONESS
Introducing: Vera the VIPER, Chuck the CHIMP, and Dave
        the DINGO

And Including:

Barbara BEAR	Bella BLACKBIRD	Bluesy the BLUE JAY
Edd the EEL	Ethan the ELEPHANT	Gideon the GIRAFFE
Harvey the HYENA	Helda the HEN	Henry the HORSE
Molly the MONKEY	Randy ROOSTER	Redd ROBIN
Rita the RABBIT	Sassy SQUIRREL	Warren the WOLF
and Featuring:	Paul-is-the-WALRUS	

References

1 The Beatles. "Strawberry Fields Forever." Magical Mystery Tour, Parlophone, 1967

2 The Beatles. "Norwegian Wood (This Bird Has Flown)." Rubber Soul, Parlophone, 1965.

3 A.J. Perez, "The Chicago Cubs Billy Goat Curse, Explained, 2016, https://www.usatoday.com/story/sports/mlb/2016/10/25/chicago-cubs-billy-goat-curse-explained/92715898/.

4 Otis Redding. "(Sittin' On) The Dock of the Bay." Volt, 1968.

5 Beach Boys. "Warmth of the Sun." Shut Down Volume 2, Capitol, 1964.

6 A Wild Hare. Avery, Tex, Warner Bros., 1940

7 John Lennon. "Imagine." John Lennon, Apple, 1971.

8 Field of Dreams. Robinson, Phil, Universal, 1989.

9 The Beatles. "Yellow Submarine." Revolver, Parlophone, 1966.

10 The Beatles. "Being for the Benefit of Mr. Kite." Sgt. Pepper's Lonely Hearts Club Band, Parlophone, 1967.

11 The Beatles. "Love You Too." Revolver, Parlophone, 1966.

12 The Beatles. "Rocky Raccoon." The Beatles ("White Album"), Apple, 1968.

13 The Beatles. "She Said, She Said." Revolver, Parlophone, 1966.

14 The Beatles. "I'm Only Sleeping." Revolver, Parlophone, 1966.

15 The Beatles. "I Want To Tell You." Revolver, Parlophone, 1966.

16 The Beatles. "Across The Universe." Let It Be, Apple, 1970.

17 The Beatles. "She's Leaving Home." Sgt. Pepper's Lonely Hearts Club Band, Parlophone, 1967.

18 The Beatles. "Lucy in the Sky with Diamonds" Sgt. Pepper's Lonely Hearts Club Band, Parlophone, 1967.

19 The Beatles. "Penny Lane." Sgt. Pepper's Lonely Hearts Club Band, Parlophone, 1967.

20 Jerry Lee Lewis. "Great Balls of Fire.", Jamboree, Sun, 1957

21 Simon and Garfunkel. "The Sound of Silence." Wednesday Morning, 3 A.M., Columbia, 1965.

22 The Rolling Stones. "Paint it, Black." Aftermath, Decca, 1966.

23 The Beatles. "Lucy in the Sky with Diamonds." Sgt. Pepper's Lonely Hearts Club Band, Parlophone, 1967.

24 Funny Girl. Wyler, William, Columbia, 1968.

25 The Beatles. "I'm Only Sleeping." Revolver, Parlophone, 1966.

26 Paul and Linda McCartney. "Uncle Albert/Admiral Halsey." Ram, Capitol, 1971.

27 The Moody Blues. "Nights in White Satin." Days of Future Passed, Deram, 1967.

28 The Tonight Show Starring Johnny Carson. de Cordova, Fred, NBC, 1963-1992.

29 Heinlein, Robert. Stranger in a Strange Land, G.B. Putnam's Sons, 1961.

30 Apollo 13. Howard, Ron, Universal, 1995.

31 Buffalo Springfield. "On the Way Home." Last Time Around, Atco, 1968.

32 The Beatles. "Fixing a Hole." Sgt. Pepper's Lonely Hearts Club Band, Parlophone, 1967.

33 The Beach Boys. Pet Sounds, Capitol, 1966.

34 The Coasters. "Yakety Kay." The Coasters, Atco, 1968.

35 E.T. the Extra-Terrestrial. Spielberg, Stephen, Universal, 1982.

36 The Beatles. "Rocky Raccoon." The Beatles ("White Album"), Apple, 1968.

37 The Beatles. "When I'm 64." Sgt. Pepper's Lonely Hearts Club Band, Parlophone, 1967.

38 The Beatles. "I am the Walrus." Magical Mystery Tour, Parlophone, 1967.

39 The Beatles. "Tomorrow Never Knows." Revolver, Parlophone, 1966.

40 The Byrds. "Turn! Turn! Turn!." Turn! Turn! Turn!, Columbia, 1965.

Billy the Baaad Goat: The Big Yellow Rocket Ship
Lewis, Mitchell, A.
Copyright 2022
ISBN:
978-0-2288-3054-2 (Hardcover)
978-0-2288-3053-5 (Paperback)
978-0-2288-3055-9 (eBook)

In most cases, names and small details have been changed to protect the identity of the animals and people involved. Any resemblance to a specific real person or animal the reader may know is purely coincidental.

The views and opinions expressed by the animals or humans featured in this book are theirs and theirs alone, and do not necessarily, but might, represent the views and opinions of the author, Grampa Mitch.

Printing 10 9 8 7 6 5 4 3 2 1
DETERMINATION